YOU ARE THE FIRST KID ON MARS

PATRICK O'BRIEN

G. P. Putnam's Sons

Would you like to go to Mars? Would you
like to ride a rocket to another world, a mysterious
red planet millions of miles from Earth? No one has
been there yet, but someday it might be possible.
This book will tell you what would happen, and
what you would do, if you were the first kid on Mars.

Mars is a cold place. A dusty, rocky, windy place. But many people are drawn by the urge to explore this strange new world. Perhaps they will even find some kind of alien life.

Someday humans might travel to Mars and set up a colony, a group of people who live and work together. Scientists, engineers, astronauts and their families might one day live on the planet Mars.

If you go to Mars, the first part of your trip might be on a space elevator. When you arrive at the Earth station, you see the very, very long cables that are anchored to the ground and go straight up all the way into space. There, they are attached to a space station.

■ The elevator car travels up and down the cables, bringing people and supplies to and from space.

■ As you travel up in the elevator car, you watch out the window as the blue sky gradually turns to starry black. You are in space.

■ The climber stops, and you crawl through a hatch and into the space station. There is no gravity in space, so you float through the air, lighter than a feather.

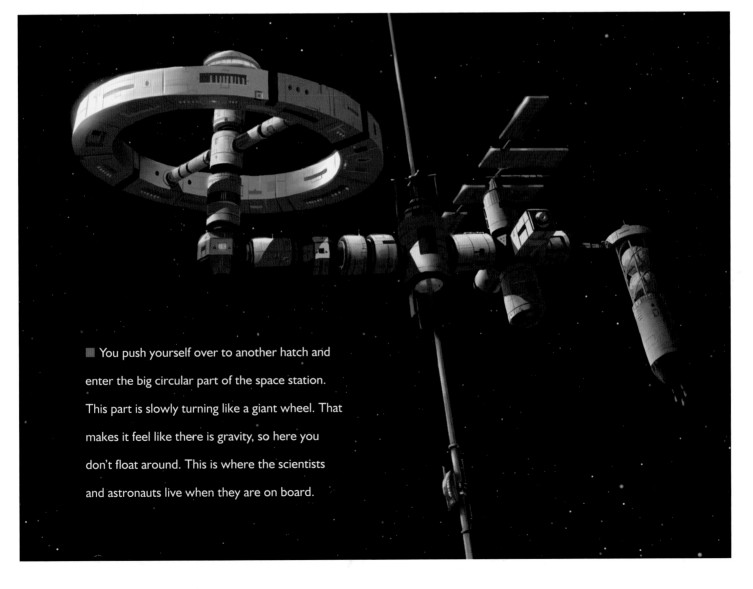

■ You push yourself over to another hatch and enter the big circular part of the space station. This part is slowly turning like a giant wheel. That makes it feel like there is gravity, so here you don't float around. This is where the scientists and astronauts live when they are on board.

The rocket that will take you to Mars is docked at the space station. It's powered by a new kind of engine called a Nuclear Thermal Rocket, and it goes much faster than the space shuttles and the moon rockets did. You climb aboard and take a seat.

The launch is slow and smooth, and gradually the rocket builds up speed until it is going more than 75,000 miles per hour. You're on your way.

The rocket speeds through space toward Mars, and you settle in for a long trip. Even though Mars is the closest planet to Earth, it is still a very long way away. As Earth and Mars each travel around the sun, they are sometimes as close as 35 million miles to each other, and sometimes as far as 248 million miles from each other. The rocket to Mars travels when the planets are closest together, but even so, it will take about four months to get there.

Seen from Earth, Mars looks like a red point of light. For this reason, people often call it "the red planet."

The rooms in the ship are small and crowded, but you and the crew have everything you need. This part of the ship is spinning, so it feels like there is gravity. There's a small kitchen and tiny bathrooms. There's an exercise room that is also a TV room and a library.

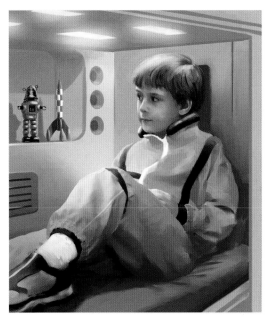

In the sleeping cabin, you are on the top bunk, where you have a small compartment to keep all the things you have brought for the trip.

Out the window you can see Earth. It seems very small now, just a tiny part of the huge universe.

As the weeks pass, Mars is getting larger and larger in your window, until at last, the dry, rocky surface fills your view. You see a space station floating above the planet. That's the Mars orbital base. Slowly, carefully, the rocket docks with the base.

The orbital base stays in orbit above Mars. A ship called the Mars Lander is docked to it. The lander takes people down to the planet and back.

Climb aboard the lander and buckle up—it's going to be a bumpy ride.

The lander detaches from the orbiter and heads down to the surface.

The lander enters the thin air above Mars at about 15,000 miles per hour. You feel the ship shaking and jerking, and you see flames shooting past the window. The Martian air is slowing you down. Then the flames stop and you are plummeting toward the surface.

To slow the fall, large parachutes pop out of the nose of the ship, and you feel a sharp jolt as they open. Then a rocket engine fires beneath the ship to slow it down, and the crew brings it to a soft landing on the planet Mars.

Put on your space suit.

It's time to walk on Mars.

You can't go out on the surface of Mars without a space suit. There's not enough oxygen to breathe, and it is much too cold. You carry your air in tanks on your back, and your suit keeps you warm. Gravity on Mars is less than half as strong as on Earth, so you take big, bouncing steps.

You walk over to the Mars habitat and enter the air lock. This habitat will be your home on Mars.

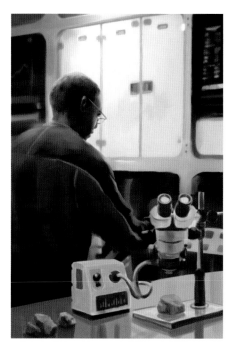

■ There are also engineers who keep the computers running, and pilots who fly the ships.

■ There are many people living in the habitat. Most of them are scientists who are studying the Martian air and rocks and water.

■ You have your own very small room.

■ Plants are being grown in a greenhouse. This part of the habitat doesn't have hard walls. It is inflated with air like a balloon. Plants are grown for food, but they also help to create the air that you are breathing, since they make oxygen in their leaves.

The scientists' most important mission on Mars is the search for Martian life. Many people think that some kind of life-form might exist on the red planet. Or perhaps something lived there long ago.

■ You have seen lots of movies with Martians, and they look like this . . .

■ or this . . .

■ or this.

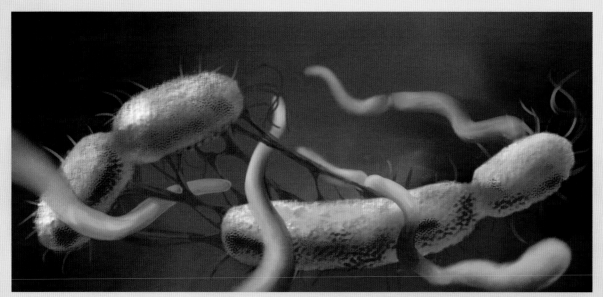

■ But if there really are living things on Mars, they would probably look more like this. You would need a microscope to see them.

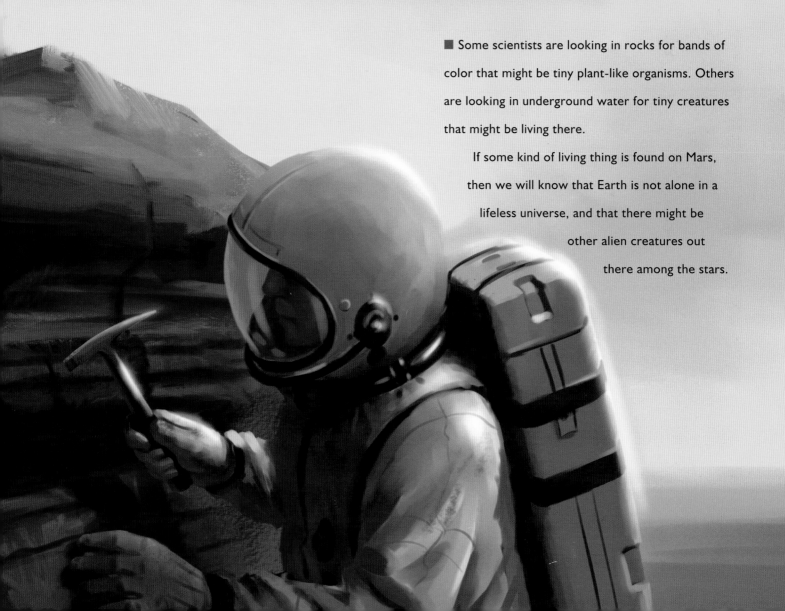

■ Some scientists are looking in rocks for bands of color that might be tiny plant-like organisms. Others are looking in underground water for tiny creatures that might be living there.

If some kind of living thing is found on Mars, then we will know that Earth is not alone in a lifeless universe, and that there might be other alien creatures out there among the stars.

The north pole of Mars is covered by a huge ice cap. It's mostly made of water. Without the water on Mars, it would not be possible for people to live on the planet.

There is also water deep under the ground. Engineers have dug wells to get water for the Mars colony. Water is needed for drinking, of course, and for growing food in the greenhouse. But it is also used in special machines to make the air that you are breathing. Another machine uses water to make the rocket fuel that you will need to get back home.

Mars can be a very windy planet. Many times small whirlwinds called dust devils sweep through the colony. They're like small tornadoes, picking up dry dirt as they go.

Sometimes strong winds howl over the landscape, filling the air with swirling dust and dirt. These huge dust storms can be so big that the whole planet is covered in a reddish haze.

There are many robot helpers on Mars. They do jobs that are too difficult or dangerous for humans to do. Sometimes they do jobs that humans find just too boring.

■ This robot rover ranges far across the Martian landscape, collecting dirt and rocks for study.

■ The robotic plane can explore even farther, sending pictures back to the scientists.

■ Robotic arms help in the greenhouse.

■ And these robots are helping to build another habitat building.

One day, you join a group of scientists on an expedition. Driving over miles of Martian soil, you watch the strange red landscape go by. Then you see a small metal object in the distance. The driver steers for it and you all get out.

It's the Sojourner, the first Mars rover. It has been sitting here quietly since it landed way back in 1997. It did some of the earliest exploring on Mars, long before humans were able to come to the planet.

It's almost time to return home, but before you go, you have time for a quick flight in the MarsPlane. This plane is specially designed to fly in the thin Martian air.

There's a huge mountain up ahead. That's Olympus Mons, the tallest mountain on any known planet. It's three times taller than Mount Everest, the tallest mountain on Earth. It's so tall that if you were on the top, you would almost be in space.

Then you explore a big canyon—a very big canyon. It's about 2,500 miles long and as much as five miles deep. That's about ten times longer and five times deeper than the biggest canyon on Earth, the Grand Canyon. This enormous crack in the Martian surface is called the Valles Marineris.

You have been on the red planet for six months, and you are looking forward to going home. Earth and Mars are moving closer together again, and the rocket is being readied for takeoff. You climb aboard to begin your long journey back to Earth. The rocket engine fires with a mighty roar, and the lander lifts off and climbs into the Martian sky.

You watch the red landscape fall away
below you as you leave Mars behind. You
have had an incredible adventure. You
have gone where no kid has gone before.
You were the first kid on Mars.

Mars is the closest planet to Earth.

Mars travels in a big circle around the sun, always staying about 140 million miles away from it. Earth travels in a smaller circle about 90 million miles from the sun.

When Earth and Mars are on opposite sides of the sun, the two planets can be as much as 248 million miles from each other. When they are both on the same side of the sun, they can be as close as 35 million miles to each other.

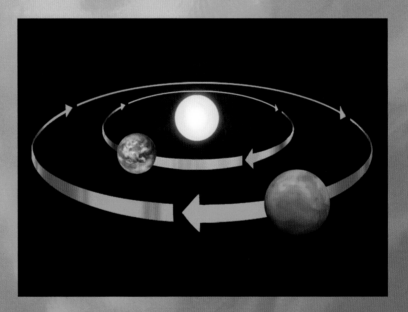

If you could travel to Mars in a car, driving at highway speed, it would take more than 60 years to get there.

Mars is about 4,200 miles in diameter, while Earth is about 8,000 miles in diameter.

Mars is much colder than Earth because it is farther from the sun. The temperature is an average of about 80 degrees below zero Fahrenheit.

It takes Mars 687 days to travel around the sun, so a Martian year is 687 days long.

Mars revolves just a little more slowly than Earth, so a day on Mars is a bit longer than an Earth day. A day on Mars is 24 hours and 38 minutes.

Mars has two tiny moons called Phobos and Deimos. They are not round, but are uneven lumps of rock. Phobos is about 17 miles wide and has a 6-mile-wide crater in the surface. Deimos is about half as big.

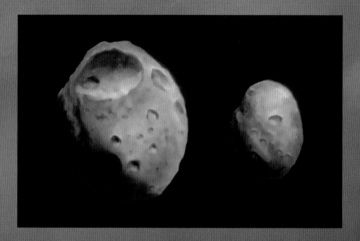

When seen from Earth, Mars looks like a bright reddish star. But like the other planets, it moves very slowly against the background of stars.

The name Mars comes from the ancient Romans. They named the planet after their god of war. Perhaps this was because the planet's red color reminded them of blood.

To Alex, my own spaceboy

■

G. P. PUTNAM'S SONS A division of Penguin Young Readers Group. Published by The Penguin Group. Penguin Group (USA) Inc., 375 Hudson Street, New York, NY 10014, U.S.A. Penguin Group (Canada), 90 Eglinton Avenue East, Suite 700, Toronto, Ontario M4P 2Y3, Canada (a division of Pearson Penguin Canada Inc.). Penguin Books Ltd, 80 Strand, London WC2R 0RL, England. Penguin Ireland, 25 St. Stephen's Green, Dublin 2, Ireland (a division of Penguin Books Ltd.). Penguin Group (Australia), 250 Camberwell Road, Camberwell, Victoria 3124, Australia (a division of Pearson Australia Group Pty Ltd). Penguin Books India Pvt Ltd, 11 Community Centre, Panchsheel Park, New Delhi - 110 017, India. Penguin Group (NZ), 67 Apollo Drive, Rosedale, North Shore 0632, New Zealand (a division of Pearson New Zealand Ltd). Penguin Books (South Africa) (Pty) Ltd, 24 Sturdee Avenue, Rosebank, Johannesburg 2196, South Africa. Penguin Books Ltd, Registered Offices: 80 Strand, London WC2R 0RL, England.

Library of Congress Cataloging-in-Publication Data: O'Brien, Patrick. You are the first kid on Mars / by Patrick O'Brien. p. cm. 1. Mars (Planet)—Exploration—Juvenile literature. 2. Mars (Planet)—Geology—Juvenile literature. 3. Life on other planets—Juvenile literature. I. Title. QB641.O27 2009 919.9'2304—dc22 2008029486 ISBN 978-0-399-24634-0   10 9 8 7 6 5 4 3 2